First published in the USA by Philomel Books,
an imprint of Penguin Random House LLC, in 2023
First published in the United Kingdom by
HarperCollins *Children's Books* in 2023

HarperCollins *Children's Books* is a division
of HarperCollins*Publishers* Ltd
1 London Bridge Street, London SE1 9GF

www.harpercollins.co.uk

HarperCollins*Publishers*
Macken House, 39/40 Mayor Street Upper
Dublin 1, D01 C9W8, Ireland

10 9 8 7 6 5 4 3 2 1

Text copyright © Drew Daywalt 2023
Illustrations copyright © Oliver Jeffers 2023
Design by Rory Jeffers

Published by arrangement with Philomel,
an imprint of Random House LLC

ISBN: 978-0-00-856082-9

Printed in Latvia

The CRAYONS GO BACK TO SCHOOL

HI!

THIS WAY

GOLD

PURPLE

DREW DAYWALT OLIVER JEFFERS

HarperCollins *Children's Books*

Summer's over,
and the crayons are
going back to school.

Blue and Beige wave
goodbye to the beach.

The night before
the first day of school
can be very exciting.

WHAT AM I GOING
TO WEAR?

And it's nice to
see old friends.

OH MY GOODNESS!
Have you got taller?

No, but You're
    looking marvellous!

And make new friends too.

HI. I'm CHUNKY Toddler Crayon.

Hi, Chunky.
I'm JUMBO Toddler Crayon.

OH, WOW! SAme last nAme!
I wonder if we're RElated!

And being busy
is fun!

Purple crayon
loves maths!

$$1 + 1 = 2$$

GOODNESS GRACIOUS ME.
MATHS IS ALWAYS SO
MUCH FUN!

Black crayon
loves writing!

I'll start with An outline.

White crayon
loves reading!

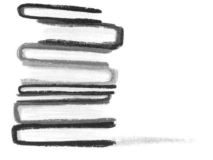

Yellow and Orange love science!

Hey, look! Jupiter is yellow AND orange!

And they're all excited
for art lessons!

Even if they
make a mess.

Actually…

ESPECIALLY if they make a mess!